COMMANDER IN CHEESE

The Big Move

D0088842

Read all the Commander in Cheese adventures!

COMMANDER IN CHEESE

The Big Move

1

Lindsey Leavitt • Illustrated by A. G. Ford

A STEPPING STONE BOOK™

Random House 🏠 New York

This is a work of fiction. Names, characters, places, and incidents either are the product of the author's imagination or are used fictitiously. Any resemblance to actual persons, living or dead, events, or locales is entirely coincidental.

Text copyright © 2016 by Lindsey Leavitt, LLC
Cover art and interior illustrations copyright © 2016 by A. G. Ford

Photo permissions: pg. 84–89 president portraits, pg. 91 Amelia Earhart and President Coolidge, and pg. 94 inaugural address from the collection of the Library of Congress Prints and Photographs Division online at www.loc.org. pg. 90 Taft bath © Granger, NYC—All rights reserved. pg. 92 Obama © AP Photo/Scott Andrews, Pool. pg. 96 moving van © Clinton Presidential Library.

All rights reserved. Published in the United States by Random House Children's Books, a division of Penguin Random House LLC, New York.

Random House and the colophon are registered trademarks and A Stepping Stone Book and the colophon are trademarks of Penguin Random House LLC.

Visit us on the Web!
SteppingStonesBooks.com
randomhousekids.com

Educators and librarians, for a variety of teaching tools,
visit us at RHTeachersLibrarians.com

Library of Congress Cataloging-in-Publication Data
Names: Leavitt, Lindsey, author. | Ford, AG, illustrator.
Title: The big move / Lindsey Leavitt ; illustrated by AG Ford.
Description: New York : Random House, [2016] | Series: Commander in Cheese ; 1 |
"A Stepping Stone Book." | Summary: "Mice siblings who live in the White House prepare for a new president to move in"—Provided by publisher.
Identifiers: LCCN 2015027161 | ISBN 978-1-101-93112-7 (paperback) |
ISBN 978-1-101-93113-4 (hardcover library binding) | ISBN 978-1-101-93114-1 (ebook)
Subjects: | CYAC: Mice—Fiction. | Brothers and sisters—Fiction. | Presidents—Family—Fiction. | White House (Washington, D.C.)—Fiction. | Humorous stories. |
BISAC: JUVENILE FICTION / Animals / Mice, Hamsters, Guinea Pigs, etc. |
JUVENILE FICTION / People & Places / United States / General. | JUVENILE FICTION / Humorous Stories.
Classification: LCC PZ7.L46553 Bi 2016 | DDC [E]—dc23
LC record available at http://lccn.loc.gov/2015027161

Printed in the United States of America
10 9 8 7 6 5 4 3 2

This book has been officially leveled by using
the F&P Text Level Gradient™ Leveling System.

Random House Children's Books supports the First Amendment
and celebrates the right to read.

To my Brudes: Brett, Zach, and Morgan

★ ★ ★ ★ ★ ★ ★ ★ ★ ★

Ava and Dean were like any other sister and brother. They had dance contests. They fought over the last piece of pizza. They read together. Their favorite book was *If You Give a Mouse a Cookie*. One time, Dean accidentally hit Ava in the nose with a ball.

Normal sibling stuff.

If you're a human, Ava and Dean could fit in your hand. If you're a mouse, then you might know about Ava and Dean Squeakerton. They *are* kind of famous, for mice.

That's because Ava, Dean, and the rest of

their family live in the White House. Yes, THAT White House. Also the home of the president of the United States of America.

Over forty human presidents have moved in and out of the White House. The Squeakerton family has lived there since 1800, the same year President John Adams moved in. That's more than two hundred years of mouse memories, stories, and hiding. Lots of hiding.

If you're a human, you should also know that mice are very smart animals. Definitely smarter than hippos, but don't tell any hippos that.

Mice are a lot like humans.

They have homes, families, and hobbies.

They build interesting burrows.

They squeak beautiful music.

But humans are busy living their human lives. They don't notice this whole mouse world happening right by their stinky human feet.

Until now.

As a human would say, the cat is out of the bag. (A mouse would never say that, of course. Mice don't say the c-a-t word unless they are screaming and running away.)

That means the top-secret information is out. The information that should not be written in a book. If you must blame someone for spilling these secrets, DO NOT blame this book.

Blame Ava and Dean. They almost blew it for everyone. And of course there was a c-a-t involved in the whole mess. . . .

Moving day! It's an exciting and scary day for anyone. But for Ava and Dean Squeakerton, this day was really hard. And it wasn't even *their* moving day.

Today the new president and her family would make the White House their home. Furniture would be moved around. Boxes had to be unpacked, and different food stored in the kitchen.

The old president moving out and the new president moving in, all within a few short hours!

"I wish the other candidate won," Ava said as Dean nibbled on a piece of cheddar cheese. They were sitting at the counter in the mouse kitchen.

The Squeakerton family lived in secret rooms throughout the house. Some rooms were over seventy years old, burrowed when President Truman redid the White House in 1948.

The humans had no clue there was a large mouse colony living right beside them. Did I mention mice are smart?

"You said that guy looked mean," Dean said.

"He did. I bet he would have stomped around all the time. He looks like a stomper." Ava twirled her tail around her finger. "And I do like President Caroline Abbey. She'll do a good job doing whatever human presidents do. I just wish her kids were grown up already."

"I'm glad she has kids. Kids make it more

fun," Dean said. He swallowed his cheese with a loud gulp. He loved cheese. "The boy is seven, just like you, and the girl is nine, just like me. All the other mice think it's perfect."

"If all the other mice jumped off a cliff, would you?" Ava asked.

"If I was a lemming, I might. Lemmings are followers," Dean said. "Which is why I'm glad I'm a mouse."

Libby, the main mouse cook, hummed a tune as she squeezed past them. She wasn't very good at humming. Most mice aren't. "Put the orange juice away when you're done!" she called.

Ava sipped her juice from a ChapStick tube. She liked this spot in the kitchen because Libby treated them like normal kids.

Their dad, Mr. James F. Squeakerton, was in charge of the mice living in the White House. Sort of like the president. Ava and Dean's

great-great-great-great-great-great-great-great-(this can take forever—count fifty-seven greats)-grandpa was sort of like a president too. He started a radio broadcast in the White House press room. Humans don't speak mouse, so it was an excellent way for mice around the country to communicate. The Squeakertons saved many lives by squeaking all sorts of warnings and advice over the years.

So being a Squeakerton was a big deal in the mouse world. But sometimes a mouse just needed to feel like any other mouse. Being told to put the juice away felt like something any house mouse in America would hear.

Dean bit into a chunk of bread. The Squeakertons got most of their food from the trash area. You would be surprised how much perfectly good human food was thrown out in the White House.

"I bet the boy has cool toys," Dean said.

"What do you care? It's not like you'll ever get to see his toys," Ava said.

"Maybe I will," Dean said. "Maybe I'll sneak up there today and look at the boy's room."

Ava stopped sipping her juice. "But the boy's room is on the second floor."

There were tunnels that led the animals to their mini rooms. The mice had built rooms into the walls of the White House kitchen, the library, even the Oval Office. The Squeakertons' bedrooms, classrooms, and living areas were burrowed in the basement.

But there wasn't a tunnel to the kids' rooms. Mice stayed away from the second floor. That was where the president's family lived. Even mice knew the president needed a private space.

"I'll tell Mom if you go," Ava said.

"No, you won't. If you tell Mom about that,

I'll tell her about the time you snuck into the State Dining Room looking for dress beads," Dean said.

Ava shook her head. "I found two, and she won't even care."

Libby brushed past them again. "That's enough cheddar for you, mister."

Dean pushed away his plate. He was too excited to eat anyway.

"We get to see the inauguration today. That's the event where the new president becomes official," Ava said. "Most mice would rather see that than look for toys."

"We aren't most mice," Dean said. He hopped out of his seat. "Think of the Treasure Rooms, Ava. We have bits of things from tons of presidents. It's a room full of history. But what are we missing?"

"A statue of a brother who listens to his little sister?" Ava suggested.

"No. Think of the toy section. The building section. Ava, what if we found . . . a . . . a you-know-what?"

"Don't say it! We don't even know if they're real."

"They are," Dean said. "Ava, I am going on a quest! I will find . . . a . . . Lego!"

"What? A Lego?" Ava glanced around the room to make sure no one was listening. Had her brother gone CRAZY? "That's not going to happen."

"What if we found one? No one has added something that exciting to the Treasure Rooms since George Washington's ivory teeth. We would be legends!"

Ava liked adventure. But she didn't dream about unicorns traveling on rainbows. She did not believe that c-a-t-s were ever nice to mice. That stuff wasn't real. And since no mouse in the White House had ever seen a Lego, they had no idea if the toy was real.

"I mean, we probably wouldn't find a Lego," Ava said. "But we do have the day off from school. If we wanted to take something, moving day would be a good time to do it."

"Right. The kids will think it got lost in the move. We need more toys in the Children's Collection," Dean said.

Ava nodded. "Those green army men get boring after a while."

"See?" Dean's whiskers twitched with excitement. "Aunt Agnes will be so proud that we found something new. Something different."

"Aunt Agnes would be excited. . . ." Ava loved surprising her favorite aunt. "I just don't know if it's a good idea. There are so many people here. Someone will see."

Dean bounced up and down. "I'm going. I

bet the boy has a million Legos. I heard you can build all sorts of things. Towers. Mansions. Maybe I will move into a Lego house for a whole night."

"You wouldn't do that," Ava said.

Dean shrugged. "Everyone will be so glad we have a Lego in the collection. It's okay if you don't come with me. I can bring you a pink one."

Ava tugged at her brother's tail. "Yellow!

You know yellow is my favorite color. Ugh, you are just going to mess this up. Fine. I'll take you up there."

Ava loved adventure—she really did. Especially with her brother. Especially if it was for a good cause. Nothing would be more exciting than adding a Lego to the Treasure Rooms. Not even a presidential inauguration could top that. "Now you follow me. I know these tunnels like the back of my claw."

Ava took Dean to the Treasure Rooms. The rooms were already full of neat stuff. Ava and Dean wanted to make sure the Lego would have a good spot.

The Squeakerton family had collected presidential treasures for hundreds of years. They had shoehorns, toothbrushes, and tools. Some of the items were just for looks. Some stuff they used. Ava liked to take a bath in the gravy boat from Jacqueline Kennedy's china set.

"A Lego would be much cooler than Lyndon Johnson's toenail clippers," Ava said.

"Should we try to find some other keepsakes because it's an important day? See if we can get a presidential pin? No one has found a good pin in a while." Dean pushed one of James Madison's wooden buttons to the side. Mice are very strong, by the way. They make ants look like puny snails. "Maybe if we got rid of the old scarves—"

Ava squeaked. "Do not touch the scarves!"

Ava loved fabric. Any print. Any texture. Lace, tweed, cotton. Lined up in the Treasure Rooms were scraps of clothing from every First Lady. A silver bead from Caroline Harrison's red evening gown was Ava's favorite item.

"Fine," Dean grumbled. "Let's head into the Children's Collection."

The Treasure Rooms were a series of rooms that were joined together, sort of like a museum.

There was the Grooming and Clothing Collection, where they kept combs and hats. The Stuff We Use Collection was pretty easy to understand. It was the biggest room.

The Children's Collection had not been added to in a while. The previous president's children were grown up. In fact, the only time Ava and Dean had actually seen children was on tours or at holiday events, like the Easter Egg Roll on the White House lawn.

Ava and Dean grabbed a mousepack hanging from a hook.

Every mouse had a different job. Some mice were Takers, and they picked up discarded or lost things for the mice to use. Takers always wore a mousepack, just in case they found something useful. Dean and Ava were not Takers, but maybe that would be their job when they grew up.

Dean pointed to the empty spaces. "If we get one Lego, we can put it there. But what if we find enough to build with?"

Dean loved to build. He had built all the furniture in their family's house using odds and ends. He wanted to build a bridge across the National Mall someday.

"We do not know the size of a Lego," Ava said. She smoothed out her tail. "Let's go up there and see first. Maybe there are no Legos."

"Maybe there are a million," Dean said. "But you're right. We better go now, before someone sees us leave."

They scurried out of the Treasure Rooms and ran right into a large mouse. "Just where do you think you're going?" he asked.

It was their third cousin Gregory. Of course it was Gregory. Any time Ava and Dean went looking for adventure, Gregory blocked them.

He was like their Secret Service agent *and* nanny.

"Did I hear you say *Lego*?" Gregory asked. Gregory wore a black suit and black sunglasses. Gregory was the largest mouse in the house. If he didn't have such a thin tail, you would think he was a rat.

Warning: Gregory did not like being called a rat.

"*Lego?* No one said *Lego*," Dean said. "We said . . . *gego*."

"He means *gecko*," Ava said. She rolled her eyes at her brother. "We heard the president might get a gecko for a pet."

There was always a lot of talk about the new president's pets. The president usually got a dog. If the mice were unlucky, a c-a-t.

Gregory twitched his nose. "Great. Reptiles. Not safe. Why are you wearing mousepacks?"

Ava shrugged. "In case we find an interesting rock on the roof."

"Oh. Okay." Gregory shook his head. "Look, today is a crazy day, so I'm in charge of you. Please get your coats on. We're going to watch the inauguration from the roof."

"Oh, is it time already?" Dean asked. "Can we be a little late?"

Gregory held up his claw. "We have a new commander in chief."

"Do you mean commander in cheese?" Dean asked.

Gregory shook his head. "The human president is called our commander in chief. And when a new one starts, it is your duty to be there. This is an important day in history."

"Every day is an important day in this house," Dean grumbled.

"Don't worry. The inauguration will be fun, and then we'll get the Lego," Ava whispered. "And we will be as quiet as, well, mice."

A va and Dean went up to the roof to watch the inauguration with their family. At least they got to leave the house. Sort of. The only outside places they were allowed to go were the roof and the garden.

The roof made Ava happy because she loved heights. Her biggest dream was to fly in the sky someday! She didn't like standing on a ledge and seeing all of Washington, D.C. The city was full of interesting places she would never visit. Today the streets were jammed with cars and people.

The president and the president-to-be met at the White House for tea before driving together to the ceremony. Tea meant fresh scones, which meant dessert that night for the Squeakertons.

Inauguration Day happened on January 20 on the west steps of the Capitol Building. There were speeches and music. Then Caroline Abbey would raise her right hand and become the new president.

"The people look smaller than us from here," Gregory said.

"Everyone is smaller than Gregory," Dean whispered.

Ava laughed.

The mice of the White House gathered on the southeast side. There were human bodyguards on the roof too, but their job was to make sure the president was safe. They didn't worry about animals.

The mice couldn't see the actual ceremony. A very long street called Pennsylvania Avenue connected the White House and the Capitol Building. There were people on the street and big movie screens, but mice could see only so far. Watching the ceremony would have been neat, but they had to listen on the radio. Which was ... boring. No offense.

There had been dinners and galas and

concerts for days. Tonight there would be many inaugural balls. President Abbey would start her first day of work in the morning.

The presidential motorcade left. Groups of people cheered and waved as the cars moved down the street. The white moving trucks of the new president drove in right away. The staff had only a few hours to unpack.

"Where is your scarf?" Mr. Squeakerton asked Dean.

Dean tried not to shiver. "Inside."

"I guess you shouldn't make fun of the scarf collection," Ava said.

Mr. Squeakerton squinted at the morning sun. "Can you run inside and get some warmer clothes? This will go for a long time."

"I'll run in with him!" Ava said. "Don't worry about us. With all the movers, everyone will be busy."

Mr. Squeakerton smiled. "I wish our mini camera worked. Ask Aunt Agnes about that."

"Ask Aunt Agnes what?" Their aunt scurried over. She worked near the Situation Room in the West Wing and fixed all the technology and wiring for the mice. She also found new uses for things in the Treasure Rooms. Once, she made a mini radio out of a walnut shell.

"How can we get that video camera to work again?" Mr. Squeakerton asked. "I want  to give it to the kids when they go somewhere, so we can watch what they're doing."

"Something isn't working. I'll look at it today." Agnes zipped up her hoodie. "I just fixed a laptop yesterday. I've been busy."

Ava wanted to be clever like her aunt someday. Aunt Agnes could probably think of thirty things to do with a Lego.

"Thank you for all you do, Agnes." Mr. Squeakerton hugged his sister. "The kids are just running inside for a little bit. I'm sure they'll be fine."

"Yep!" Dean said. "We will be smart little mice."

Aunt Agnes smiled. "Do you need Gregory to go with you?"

Gregory grunted. He didn't want to miss the ceremony. Gregory knew more White House facts than any mouse there.

"Don't worry, Gregory. If this speech is as long as President William Henry Harrison's, you might get to stay up here all day," Mr. Squeakerton said.

Dean and Ava were already running down the stairs. They would never have a chance to explore like this again, not ever! That Lego was going to look so cool in the Treasure Rooms.

Mice don't have laws like humans do. This is because mice pretty much follow the rules. Rules are there to help you. Laws are there because someone breaks them and then goes to jail.

There are no mice jails.

Mice understand that rules are there to protect them. Here are some very smart mice rules:

1. Do not drink water from the toilet. Humans do things in those toilets.

2. When you place droppings, try to do it

where people can't see. Humans get really upset when they find mice droppings. Droppings mean there was a mouse around, and humans don't always like mice or mice droppings. We should probably stop talking about droppings.

3. If there is more green than yellow on the cheese, don't eat it.

3½. Especially if that cheese is on a mouse trap. Okay. So some mice aren't smart.

4. The Oval Office is the best place to run for exercise. One lap is exactly one mouse mile.

5. Follow the mouse schedule. Early morning or late at night is the best time if you have to leave the tunnels.

6. And seriously. DO NOT run around the White House in the middle of the day. Especially in the middle of

MOVING day. (Okay. This isn't an actual mouse rule. But it should be!)

Dean and Ava were usually smart mice. But today they weren't. Today they left their smartness on that roof! Because there weren't tunnels to get to the kids' rooms. That meant they had to cross four rooms to get there.

Four.

Four chances to get stomped on by movers wearing boots. Big, heavy, stompy boots. Or boxes! What if a box was dropped on them, or a mirror, or that antique chair that Martin Van Buren used to sit on?

Ava and Dean ran across the Lincoln Sitting Room. This room used to be part of the president's office. Now it was just fancy chairs and sofas. There are a lot of fancy chairs in the White House.

"Mouse!" shouted a mover carrying a very expensive vase.

The boots stomped and hopped. Ava and Dean rolled behind a table with a hidden mousehole.

"Ava!" Dean yelled. "You can't run across like that! You know the saying, 'A mouse against the wall is the best mouse of all.'"

"We're on the second floor, Dean." Ava twirled her tail nervously. "We have to cross because the tunnels stopped."

"Maybe we should go back," Dean said.

"This was your idea."

"Sometimes I have bad ideas," Dean said.

"That's true."

"What if Legos aren't real?" Dean asked.

Ava shook her head. "No. They are. We are almost there. Three more rooms. We can do this."

The brother and sister zipped through the Lincoln bathroom. *Whoosh!*

They just barely missed a rug being rolled

across the floor in the East Sitting Hall. Rugs were heavy!

Ava and Dean stopped behind Woodrow Wilson's favorite urn.

"Take a deep breath." Dean slid his foot across the floor.

Ava yanked Dean's tail and pulled him back. Dean had almost run in front of a mover!

They waited for the mover to turn the corner, then *vroom!* The mice bolted through the Center Hall and into the next room.

The next room was the boy's room. Ava and Dean had gone where no mouse had gone before. Or if another mouse had, they never came back to tell anyone about it.

"You ready?" Dean whispered.

Ava nodded. Together, the two siblings slid through the small crack in the doorway.

There were boxes behind the door of the kid's bedroom. Just . . . boxes.

"What were we thinking?" Dean asked. "If there are toys, they're still packed!"

"Dean, calm down. It's fine," Ava said.

Dean flopped onto the floor. He could be a little floppy when he got upset. "No! We are missing the ceremony. We almost got stepped on. And now . . . boxes! Boxes! Boxes!"

"Please stop saying *boxes*," Ava said.

A mover pushed into the room, and Ava and Dean hurried under the bed.

"Let's just get a scarf and go back to the roof." Dean sighed. He also did some big sighs. He was a dramatic one, that mouse.

Ava watched the movers as they stacked box after box. "It's not like that stuff is staying in the boxes for long. The whole house has to be unpacked before the kids come home from the inaugural balls tonight!"

"But Gregory is going to come looking for us if we don't hurry."

"Fine." Ava was getting annoyed. "Then let's go back."

"Unless . . . we climb through the boxes?"

"Yes!" Ava said.

Dean poked his head out. The boxes were taped shut. He would have to nibble through the packaging and find a way to open the flaps. He didn't know how long it would take to go through each box. Usually he was a better planner than this. The Legos just made him so excited. "Maybe this was a bad idea."

Ava grabbed her brother's claw. "What if the great Amelia Earhart had decided flying across the Atlantic was a bad idea? She never would have come to the White House to meet President Coolidge. And we wouldn't have a piece of her chewing gum in the Treasure Rooms."

"What's the point?"

Ava peeked out from under the bed. "Squeak-ertons don't quit."

Dean sighed his last sigh. He was older, but sometimes his sister was smarter. Or maybe not smarter...bolder. Either way, they could not turn back. "You're right. Let's get through those boxes."

A mover grunted. "That's all of it. Let's go finish the library boxes. We'll unpack this room after the special package arrives."

"Special package?" Ava whispered to Dean.

The movers shuffled out of the room. But just when Ava and Dean were about to burrow into the first box, they heard the very worst sound a mouse could hear.

The door closed.

And then there was a click.

Ava and Dean were locked in a room that had no windows and no mouseholes. No tunnels.

In case you are not smart like a mouse is smart (although not these mice at this moment): Ava and Dean were STUCK!

This wasn't the first time a mouse had been stuck in a White House room. It happened all the time. Ava and Dean's twenty-sixth great-grandmother was locked in the Map Room during World War II. She was always scared of pushpins after that day. And poor Seventh-Uncle Otis drowned in President William Taft's extra-large bathtub. We probably shouldn't bring that up right now, though. Not with Ava and Dean about to cry.

But really. It was a big bathtub. You should have seen it.

"I take it back," Ava said. "This *was* a bad idea."

Dean paced. "It's not like we're locked in forever. Just...just a few hours."

"Dad is probably calling every mouse in the house to look for us," Ava cried. "And Gregory. We are going to have to listen to so many speeches from Gregory. I hope Aunt Agnes has this room wired so we can yell and they can come find us."

Dean was already climbing into a box. "Shoes. Ugh, it's a box of shoes. Wow, the boy human has stinky feet. Stinkier than most humans' feet."

"What are you doing?" Ava asked.

"Trying to solve a problem. Get into a box. Let's see if we can find something to help us."

"Why don't you just read the boxes?" Ava asked. Dean had already nibbled his way into a box of books.

Mice can read human letters. Do you know WHY they are able to do this? Because they are a word that rhymes with *dart*. (It also rhymes with a gross word that we will not mention here.)

"This one is school supplies." Ava bounced to another box. "This one is l-e-o-t-a-r-d-s? What is a *leotard*?"

"Maybe it is a kind of c-a-t," Dean whispered.

"That's a leopard," Ava said. "Not a leotard."

"Close enough."

Ava let out a squeak and tore through the cardboard. "Air . . . air . . . it's an air . . ." She jumped down and pushed the box with all her might until it toppled over. Like I said, mice are very strong. "It's an airplane!"

It was a beautiful model airplane with a remote control! Ava had seen airplanes in books. She'd seen the presidential helicopter.

But this airplane was just her size! She scrambled inside. Her tail hung out a little bit, but that was even better. Her tail could blow in the wind.

"Dean! Dean! Push those buttons. Make me fly."

Dean hopped down from his box. He didn't say anything. He knew his sister, and he knew this was a dream come true for her. She had wanted to fly as long as he knew her. The Legos could wait.

Dean pushed a button. Nothing happened. He pushed another. Still nothing. He jiggled the remote and played with the stick.

Ava shook the steering wheel. "Make it go!"

Dean flipped the remote over and opened the back. "There's no battery. It needs a small, round one."

Ava frowned. This was the closest she had ever been to flying. It was like this airplane was

made for her. "I bet there are some in the boxes. Maybe another toy?"

They dug through five more boxes. Ava wasn't very careful about keeping things neat. In fact, in fifteen minutes, the whole room was a disaster! She was no longer thinking about Legos. She didn't care that she and Dean were locked in a room. She didn't care that their parents were probably looking for them.

None of this mattered. There were only two words in Ava Squeakerton's head.

Battery and *flight*.

Finally, after what seemed like an hour, they found a box under the other boxes. It was big and heavy and hard to open. On the cardboard was a magical word.

Toys.

They found a collection of plastic zoo animals. They found an art kit with half of the paint gone. They found a sword, a doll, and a toy mouse.

There was some sort of black case that had buttons on it. Maybe another remote control. Ava didn't know or care. She ripped open the back. A battery fell out. But it was a rectangle and not right for the airplane. She knew it the second she saw it. She wanted to cry.

"Ava. Ava. Look!"

Ava hung her head. She had been so close to flying. So close. She would never have this chance ever again. She would have to sit on that roof of the great, big White House and watch the planes overhead and dream her days away. She was, after all, only a mouse. Mice are small and they probably shouldn't dream so big.

"What," Ava said. It wasn't really a question.

"A Lego!" Dean screamed.

And there it was. The object they had never

been sure existed. A whole bin filled with Legos in a rainbow of colors. There were boxes with pictures of castles and spaceships too. Dean could build every day for the rest of his life and still not use all those Legos.

The door clicked again. Dean and Ava gasped and hurried under a box.

They could see feet. HUMAN FEET.

9

Ava and Dean stayed very quiet as the human feet walked across the room.

"What happened to my room?" a boy's voice asked.

"Looks like the movers already started unpacking for you. Be glad, Banks," a girl said.

It was the president's children. Which meant...the inauguration was over! How long had Ava and Dean been in that room? Gregory had probably organized a search party for them already.

But there were Legos right in front of Ava and

Dean. And a model airplane. The two greatest toys ever invented were just within their reach.

The boy, Banks, picked up the model airplane and placed it on a dresser. "They weren't very organized about it. Good thing they didn't lose any of my Legos! Macey, did you know I have three thousand eight hundred and seventy-two?"

"You know exactly how many Legos you have?" Macey asked.

"Of course. I count them all the time. They're my favorite toy."

"You're weird," Macey said. Ava strongly agreed.

"Maybe. But I'm weird with almost four thousand Legos," Banks said. "Come on. Let's find the hat."

"I can't believe Mom made such a big deal about you wearing that hat," Macey said.

"It was her great-grandpa's. He wore it when

he was governor. It means a lot to Mom that I wear it tonight," Banks replied.

"Here it is!" Macey called from the closet. "Good thing the movers already brought in our clothes."

She stuck the gray hat on her brother's head. Ava wanted a piece of fabric from that hat. It seemed like very warm wool. They needed more wool in the Fabric Collection.

"Can you believe we're actually living in the White House?" Banks asked. "It doesn't seem real."

"I don't think I'll sleep the first week!" Macey said. "Just knowing all the people who have lived here before us . . . it's like a movie."

"The inauguration was cool. Did you see Mom's hand shaking when she got sworn in?" Banks asked.

"Well, it was really cold out. She looked relieved when it was over."

"We better hurry." Banks looked at the door. "We need to get ready for the balls. They're making me wear a suit."

"Get used to it. We'll have to dress up all the time now." Macey circled the room and stopped by the white fireplace. "Clover will LOVE it here."

"Where is Clover, anyway?" Banks asked.

"I don't know. I wouldn't leave out that airplane if she's coming. She loves airplanes."

Dean whispered to Ava, "I think I heard they have a pet guinea pig. That would be fun. You two can hop in the airplane together."

"Maybe," Ava said. The door was open. This was probably the best chance for them to sneak out. They had to get back to their family before everyone tried to find them. It wasn't safe for all those mice to run around the house looking for them. Dean and Ava loved the whole Squeakerton family and wouldn't want anything to happen to anybody. All they had wanted was one Lego. Was that too much to ask?

"We need a plan," Dean whispered.

Dean looked at Ava. Ava looked at Dean. And then it was like the plan came together without anyone saying anything. That's the good thing about having a sibling. Sometimes you don't need to say anything. You just know what the other one is thinking. And that was good. Because they both had a really, really crazy idea.

Ava and Dean had to get out of the boy's room. This was the situation:

There were six boxes between Ava and Dean and the Legos.

Then a whole empty floor.

Then, of course, all those rooms.

Did I mention how big the rooms are in the White House? Answer: very big.

Ava zigged right. Dean zagged left. Dean was spotted. Ava was not.

"It's a mouse!" Banks squealed. "Ew!"

"Cool, catch it!" Macey exclaimed. "We can make it a pet."

Ava ran to the middle of a box. She hoped the children would spot her and stop chasing Dean. But they didn't even see her! Meanwhile, Dean ran into a box. Was he getting a Lego?

"Dump out the box. Get rid of it," Banks said. "Mice are dirty."

Even though Dean was scared and stuck in a dark box, he was offended. He'd taken a bath just that morning. In an actual bathtub! He wasn't some gross c-a-t that licked itself clean.

"Hurry and tape the box shut," Macey said. "Then I can go get a cage for the mouse."

A cage? Ava didn't want her brother trapped in a cage! So she did the only thing she could think to do. She pushed a box into the boy.

"Ow!" Banks whirled around. "Hey! There's another mouse. Did it . . . did it just push a BOX on me?"

"Mice aren't strong enough to push a box! Don't be silly," Macey said. "Now, where is that tape?"

Ava climbed up the side of the box while

Macey was looking for the tape. Banks rubbed his leg.

"Dean! Psst. Come here," Ava whispered.

Dean was still searching the box. "I know it's in here somewhere."

"We already found the Legos," Ava hissed.

"I'm not looking for a Lego."

Ava turned. "Come on. Grab my tail and let's go."

Dean reached for his sister. Ava reached back. She reached too far. She fell in!

"Here's the tape!" Macey said.

"Look at this," Dean said. He held up a small, round circle. He'd found his sister a battery for the remote! "Just in case we ever get back to that airplane. I know you've always wanted to fly."

Ava almost hugged her brother. "Thank you. Now come on. We have to get out of here."

Ava and Dean burst out of the box. Packing

peanuts scattered across the floor. Macey tried to grab Dean and almost got his tail, but he somersaulted away from her. Ava picked up a blue Lego. She couldn't fly, but she would make sure her brother got his treasure.

"That mouse is trying to steal my Lego!" Banks shouted.

The boy knew exactly how many Legos he owned. He wasn't going to leave them lying around on the floor. He would be very careful now that he knew mice were trying to get his toy. This was Ava and Dean's only chance.

Ava and Dean made it to the door at the
same time. Dean was carrying the battery. Ava
clutched her Lego. They scampered down the
corridor and into the oval-shaped Yellow Room.
The Yellow Room is the living room for the
presidential family.

A secret service agent holding a large cage spotted the mice. He dropped the cage when he saw them. "Mice! Mice! There are mice in the White House?"

Ava and Dean hid behind a potted plant. They needed to get to the stairway, the tunnels, their family, and safety.

Another agent in a suit came around the corner. "Did you say something about mice? The children were saying something about mice too." She whispered into her walkie-talkie, "Code Brown. We have a Code Brown."

This was bad. Really, really bad. Ava and Dean had no idea what a Code Brown *was,* but it did NOT sound good.

11

"Code Brown! Vermin spotted. I repeat, Code Brown!"

Macey turned the corner. She did not seem concerned about the Code Brown. "Clover! There you are." She rushed over to the cage and opened it.

Guess what was inside. Just guess. I will give you a hint. It rhymes with *bat*.

"Meow," Clover said.

"Seriously?" Ava said. "We're never going to get out of this mess."

Dean took Ava's hand and gave it a squeeze.

Here's the good news:

- Ava had a blue Lego in her mousepack. The first Lego any Squeakerton had ever held. Probably.
- Dean had a battery. Sure, they didn't have the airplane that USED the battery and could never go back to the boy's room in a million years, but . . .
- They had each other.
- They were hidden behind a plant.
- They were healthy.
- They were still alive.
- For now.

The not-so-good-news:

- Clover.
- Code Brown, whatever that meant.
- They had been called vermin, a very rude thing to call a mouse.

- The president's daughter wanted to make them into pets.
- The staircase was far.
- Pretty much everything else was looking NOT SO GOOD.

Clover licked her lips.

"I think it's time we ask ourselves something," Dean said.

"I hope this isn't some speech about being a mouse or a man," Ava said.

"Of course not. We are mice. Mice who have lived in the White House with smart leaders for a very long time." Dean stood taller. Ava knew he was about to go into speech mode. They didn't really have time for speech mode. "Our forefathers came to this country for freedom! Liberty!"

"Dean. There is a cat in the same room as us. It isn't time to deliver another inaugural address!" Ava exclaimed.

"Okay. Then let's ask ourselves, what would Thomas Jefferson do?"

"He would write the mouse Declaration of Independence or some peace treaty." Ava rolled her eyes. "We don't have time for that either."

"No! Thomas Jefferson also knew that sometimes you have to give up something good for something better."

"Okay," Ava said. "I understand. We'll give them the battery."

But Dean knew the boy didn't care about the battery. He cared about the Lego.

More agents rushed into the room. "I heard we have a Code Brown?"

Macey held up her hands. "What is every-one talking about? There aren't any MICE here. That was a mouse TOY. Clover's favorite mouse toy. And look!" Macey held up a mouse squeaky toy that sort of looked like Dean. "I already found it."

"But I saw it move and go over there." An agent pointed near the potted plant.

Macey shook her head. "I promise. It was my toy. If there was a mouse, Clover would have eaten it already."

Dean almost stopped breathing.

"Who cares if there was a mouse? I think my mom and dad are much more worried about getting to the inaugural balls," Banks said.

The agents talked into their walkie-talkies some more. The one who looked like he was in charge motioned to the Abbey children. "We need to go."

Macey looked annoyed. "Okay, Graham. We're coming."

Graham was in charge of the kids. He was their Gregory!

Macey swooped Clover into her arms. The cat was looking at the plant like it was her next meal. "No food here, Clover."

Dean didn't know why the Abbey children had saved them. Maybe they were nice human kids? Did such a thing exist?

Dean made a decision to do something kind for the kids because they had saved his life. It wasn't an easy choice. His stomach actually hurt.

Dean pushed Ava's Lego across the floor. Banks hurried and picked it up.

"Thanks," Banks whispered. "The blue ones are my favorite."

Dean didn't answer. Mice can understand human languages, but humans don't speak any animal languages. Even if Dean could talk, he didn't know what to say. There weren't words for what he was feeling.

"Was that mouse wearing a dress?" Banks whispered to his sister.

The men in suits, the kids, and the c-a-t left the room. Ava and Dean stared at each other.

"Did we just lose a Lego?" Ava asked.

"Those kids saved our lives." Dean let out a heavy sigh. "Come on. Maybe there's an old mousehole in the Treaty Room."

There wasn't a mousehole. But there was a Gregory. And he didn't look happy.

"**W**HERE HAVE YOU BEEN?" Gregory asked. Clearly, he was yelling. "YOU LEFT THE TUNNELS AND RAN AROUND THE WHITE HOUSE!"

Ava rubbed her ears. When Gregory was mad, he didn't so much squeak as roar.

"I left the roof to get my scarf," Dean said. "And then we got distracted."

"There was a CODE BROWN!" Gregory said. "That's more than distracted."

"Well, we got a Lego. But then we ungot it," Ava said. "And there was this airplane."

"And a c-a-t," Dean added. "And a battery. But the kids are nice! Most-of-the-time nice. I don't think they want us to be their pet anymore."

Gregory's eyes lit up. "Wait. Did you say a battery?"

Dean held out the battery. "I got it for the airplane."

Ava sighed. "That airplane was so beautiful."

Gregory grinned. He'd been so mad a second ago, and now he looked happier than a hamster on a wheel. "Come with me. The family is going to be excited."

Gregory tapped on a wall. A hole slid open. This hole was not on the maps. Ava and Dean had never seen this hole.

"What is this?" gasped Ava.

"It's a hidden passage, of course." Gregory slipped into the tunnel. "The White House is full of secret passages."

Ava opened her mouth wide. "But why haven't we ever heard about this one?"

"Because then it wouldn't be a secret." Gregory smiled.

This tunnel wasn't fancy. There was dust and spiderwebs. Mice can live in some dingy places, but this was dirty for any mouse. They didn't have to go very far. Soon Gregory knocked on another wall. A door magically appeared again. To . . . the Treasure Rooms!

"Found them in the Treaty Room," Gregory said.

Ava and Dean blinked. Half of the family was in the room. The kids ran over and gave their dad a hug.

"What did you find?" Mr. Squeakerton asked.

"How did you know we were looking for something?" Ava asked. She thought her dad might be mad that they were gone so long.

Mr. Squeakerton brushed some dust off Dean's fur. "Gregory was following you in the secret tunnels the whole time."

"Not the whole time," Gregory mumbled. "Just the second half. And you weren't supposed to run into a c-a-t, you know."

"Don't worry about missing the inauguration. You can watch the video later." Mr. Squeakerton smiled at his children. "I could tell that you were up to some exploring, and today was the perfect day to do it. Especially if you found a good treasure."

Ava and Dean stared at each other. Gregory had been there all along. They were safe. Too bad they didn't get that Lego. Too, too bad.

"We had a Lego," Ava said. "But Dean gave it to the kids because they saved our lives."

"Very smart." Mrs. Squeakerton nodded.

"So all we got was this." Dean held up the battery.

All the mice in the room gasped.

Mr. Squeakerton took the battery. "I can't believe it. We can use this for the White House after-party tonight."

"You don't want to put it in the Treasure Rooms?" Ava asked.

"A Lego would have been a great treasure," Mr. Squeakerton said. "But *this* is priceless."

A few mice scrambled out of the room and returned with something rectangular.

"Is that the—"

"Mini camera! Yes!" Mr. Squeakerton patted the white electronic, which was about the size of a strawberry. "Cousin Vanessa found it during a quest. The camera used to be Sasha Obama's. Aunt Agnes has been working on it for a while now."

Aunt Agnes stepped forward. "There was a problem with the circuit board. I fixed that. But the battery is only used in cameras and other small electronics."

"Like the remote for an electronic plane?" Ava asked.

"Exactly. Now that we have the video camera, we can strap it on to anyone or anything and watch what's happening in different rooms! I have it all set up to the TV."

"So ... did we sort of go on a quest?" Dean asked.

"You did!" Mr. Squeakerton gave his son a hug. "There are many, many more adventures waiting for you and Ava. I'm excited to see what my little mice end up learning and exploring."

"Now let's go watch the inaugural balls on our mini TV!" Aunt Agnes exclaimed. The other mice cheered.

There were inaugural balls all over the city that night. The president herself attended at least ten. President Abbey looked regal in her purple gown. Her husband wore a tuxedo. Banks looked smart in his great-grandpa's hat. Macey wore a big gold skirt. They waved and smiled and danced. They seemed like nice kids, even if Macey wanted to turn the Squeakertons into pets.

Afterward, the president had a private party in the White House, her new home. The party gave the mice a chance to put their camera to good use.

"Gregory's hands are shaky," one of the mice complained as they watched the TV screen.

The mice had set up the camera so the image appeared on their screen. Now they could set the camera anywhere in the White House and find out what was happening. They had waited years for a chance like this!

"Of course my hands are shaky," Gregory said into his walkie-talkie. "I'm a mouse holding a tiny camera."

"Ooh, look at the lace on that dress." Ava sighed.

The new president made a joke. Her party guests laughed.

Dean yawned. It was after midnight. "Can I go to bed?"

"Do you want me to tuck you in?" Mr. Squeakerton asked.

"I'm tired too," Ava said. "You watch the party. Come on, Dean."

Two very tired mice scurried down the tunnel. They had been on a quest. They had escaped from their first c-a-t. They had seen history happen. It had been a big day. A good day.

"Someday we will have to figure out where all the hidden doors and secret passages are." Ava yawned.

"Yes." Dean stopped in front of his bedroom. "Someday. Good night, Ava."

Ava wasn't looking at her brother. She was looking past him. Into his room. She pointed her finger. "Dean. Look!"

A Lego! There was a yellow Lego in Dean's room! Underneath it was a note.

Uncle Ferdinand found this by a secret mousehole in the Yellow Room. Just don't be too nice to a human. You do not want to be a pet.
—Gregory

Underneath Gregory's mouse scratches was human handwriting in orange marker. The note simply said:

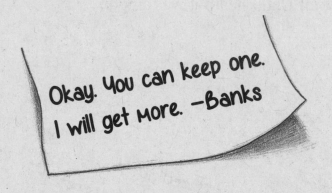

Okay. You can keep one. I will get more. —Banks

Ava and Dean smiled at each other. They didn't know why Banks had given away his treasure. They didn't know what other fun things they would find now that there were kids living nearby. They didn't know if the kids would tell anyone about the mice. It was exciting, but also dangerous.

One thing was for certain. The Abbey kids and the Squeakerton mice were ready for some adventures in their home—the beautiful White House.

The Presidents of the United States

George Washington
1789–1797

John Adams
1797–1801

Thomas Jefferson
1801–1809

James Madison
1809–1817

James Monroe
1817–1825

John Quincy Adams
1825–1829

Andrew Jackson
1829–1837

Martin Van Buren
1837–1841

William Henry
Harrison
1841

John Tyler
1841–1845

James K. Polk
1845–1849

Zachary Taylor
1849–1850

Millard Fillmore
1850–1853

Franklin Pierce
1853–1857

James Buchanan
1857–1861

Abraham Lincoln
1861–1865

Andrew Johnson
1865–1869

Ulysses S. Grant
1869–1877

Rutherford B. Hayes
1877–1881

James Garfield
1881

Chester A. Arthur
1881–1885

Grover Cleveland
1885–1889

Benjamin Harrison
1889–1893

Grover Cleveland
1893–1897

William McKinley
1897–1901

Theodore Roosevelt
1901–1909

William Howard Taft
1909–1913

Woodrow Wilson
1913–1921

Warren G. Harding
1921–1923

Calvin Coolidge
1923–1929

Herbert Hoover
1929–1933

Franklin D. Roosevelt
1933–1945

Harry S. Truman
1945–1953

Dwight D.
Eisenhower
1953–1961

John F. Kennedy
1961–1963

Lyndon B. Johnson
1963–1969

Richard M. Nixon
1969–1974

Gerald R. Ford
1974–1977

James "Jimmy"
Carter, 1977–1981

Ronald Reagan,
1981–1989

George H. W. Bush
1989–1993

William J. "Bill"
Clinton, 1993–2001

George W. Bush
2001–2009

Barack Obama
2009–

Mice Are Smart!
Three Totally Fun Facts

Very smart!

1. William Howard Taft was a large man and often had a difficult time finding a bathtub to fit his size. In fact, this bathtub was specially made for the portly president.

2. The longest inaugural address was given by William Henry Harrison. The speech took almost two hours and was delivered during a snowstorm! Harrison died from pneumonia just one month later. His term was shorter than any other American president's.

3. Amelia Earhart visited Calvin Coolidge in the White House in 1928 after becoming the first woman to fly over the Atlantic Ocean as a passenger. In 1932, she became the first woman to fly solo. Amelia Earhart was quite a celebrity in her time and was even asked to endorse

many products, including chewing gum.

Inauguration Day: Present

President Barack Obama being sworn into office on January 21, 2013, with his wife, Michelle, and daughters, Malia and Sasha, watching.

Pay attention! History is IMPORTANT!

★ Inauguration Day is January 20. (Unless it falls on a Sunday. Then it's January 21.)

★ The chief justice of the Supreme Court reads the oath of office.

★ The swearing-in ceremony starts at 11:30 sharp.

★ Speeches are given outside the Capitol Building.

★ The president gives a speech called the inaugural address.

★ Music, poetry, and prayers are also a part of the ceremony.

★ The president walks in a parade or rides back to the White House in a limousine.

★ The night ends with dozens of inaugural balls throughout Washington, D.C.

Inauguration Day: Past

A print of George Washington giving his inaugural address in April 1789.

★ The first inauguration was George Washington's in 1789. It took place in New York City on April 30. After that, Inauguration Day took place in March until 1937, when it moved to January 20.

★ In 1801, Thomas Jefferson's inauguration was the first one to be held in Washington, D.C.

★ Warren G. Harding was the first president to ride to the inauguration in a car, in 1921.

★ The first inaugural address to be televised was given by Harry S. Truman in 1949.

★ The coldest Inauguration Day was Ronald Reagan's in 1985. It was only seven degrees!

★ And John Quincy Adams was the first president to wear long trousers (pants) instead of knee breeches.

Moving Day

Presidential moving day is very busy! The presidential staff (close to one hundred people) have about five to seven hours to move out the old president's belongings and move the new president in. The day is planned out months before, and every person has a job. By the time the new president comes home, all boxes are unpacked.

The good news is, lots of the furniture stays.

The new president can also pick different furniture from a White House collection of antiques kept in storage.

The departing president and his family are often very sad to leave the staff who have served them for four to eight years. The new president has to adjust to living in the country's most famous house.

Here's a map of the floor that
Ava and Dean . . . um . . . explored.

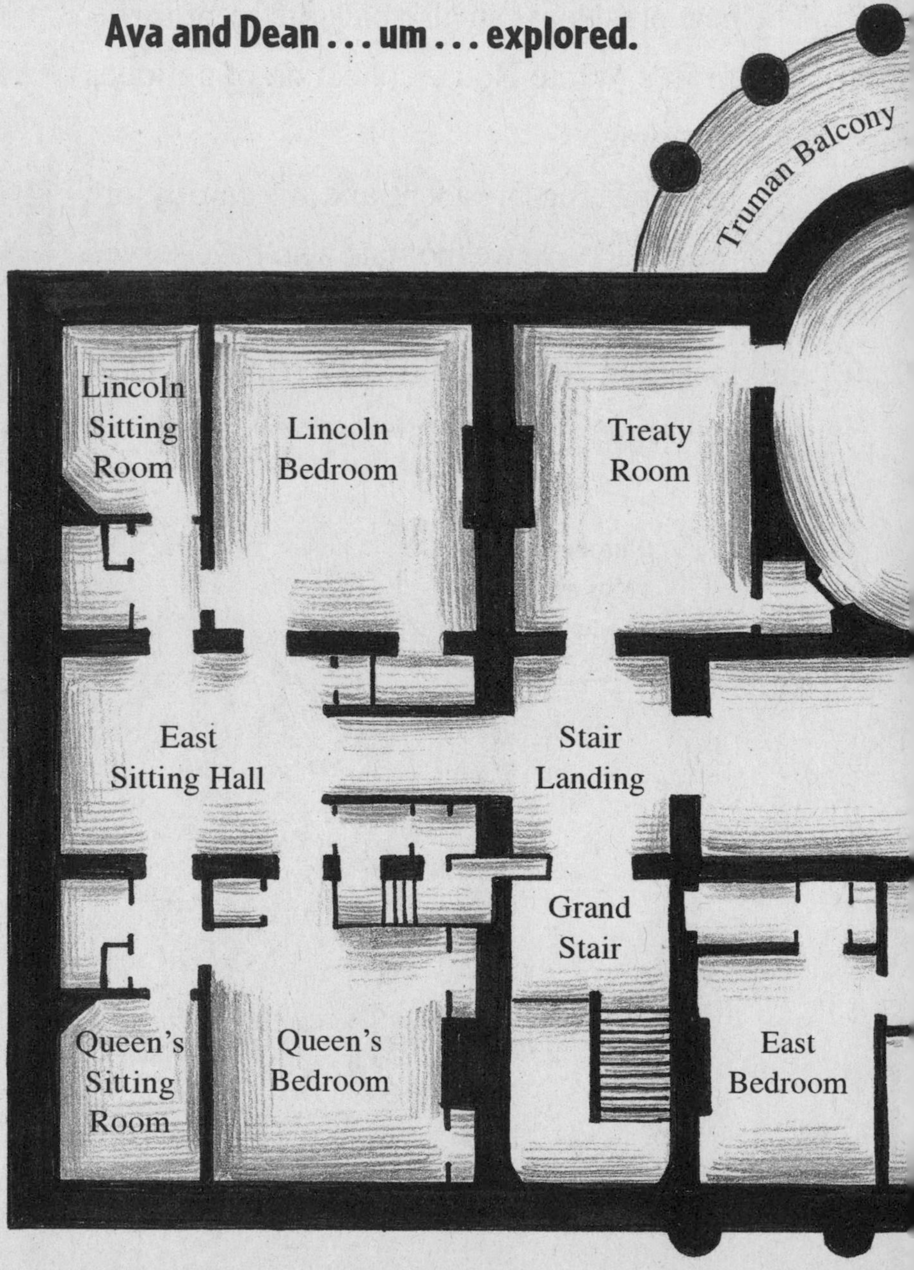

Truman Balcony

Lincoln Sitting Room

Lincoln Bedroom

Treaty Room

East Sitting Hall

Stair Landing

Grand Stair

Queen's Sitting Room

Queen's Bedroom

East Bedroom

The second floor of the White House is called the residence. Here you will find the living space and private bedrooms of the president's family. You can take a tour of the first floor of the White House. You cannot tour the second floor. In fact, the mice don't usually go up there. They respect privacy. Mostly.

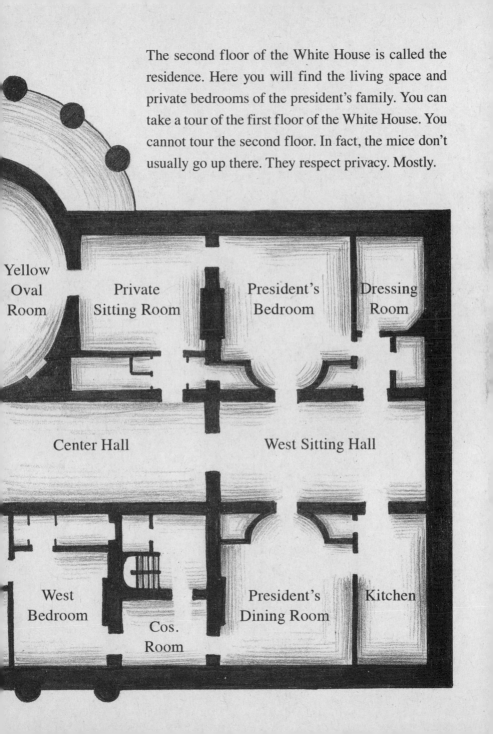

Yellow Oval Room

Private Sitting Room

President's Bedroom

Dressing Room

Center Hall

West Sitting Hall

West Bedroom

Cos. Room

President's Dining Room

Kitchen

Uh-oh!
It's time for Ava and Dean to meet the c-a-t.
Read on for a sneak peek.

Excerpt copyright © 2016 by Lindsey Leavitt, LLC.
Published by Random House Children's Books,
a division of Penguin Random House LLC, New York.

★　★　★　★　★　★　★　★　★

The Situation Room is a real room on the ground floor of the West Wing. This is where the president meets other important people to make very important decisions about the country. There is a large table and cushy office chairs. TV screens are everywhere.

That's all I can tell you. It is a TOP-SECRET room where TOP-SECRET stuff happens.

The mice had smaller rooms built into the walls of big White House rooms. The mouse Situation Room looked like the human one. Mice in military uniforms sat at the table, drinking tea. Aunt Agnes also worked in the mouse Situation Room. She dressed different than other mice. Today, she wore overalls and sandals. Sometimes she colored her ears purple.

Aunt Agnes was a computer wizard. She could fix anything. She set up microphones for the Squeakerton radio broadcast. She wired electricity in the main mouse area. She could probably make world peace if humans ever bothered to listen to animals.

Aunt Agnes waved. "Oh, good. We're all starving. That was so nice of Libby to think about us."

Dean unpacked a piece of blue cheese. Humans think blue cheese is stinky. Mice think it smells better than roses. "We didn't have any plans today. We're happy to help."

"Well, we were going to build a paper airplane," Ava said. She loved to fly, and Dean loved to build. They were a good brother-and-sister team.

"Just as long as you stay out of trouble." Gregory stacked some berries and bread onto the table. "That should be enough food for everyone."

"We just never know what to expect when a new president starts," Aunt Agnes explained. "We heard she's already having a meeting in the Oval Office."

"Do you think she'll be a nice president?" Ava asked.

"Nice isn't a problem. I just like clean and organized. Humans can be dirty animals," Aunt Agnes said.

"Can we watch the meeting?" Dean asked.

Gregory snorted. "Of course not. The Oval Office is the most famous office in the country. We don't enter when there are humans around."

Gregory ruined fun before it even started. In fact, ruining fun *was* fun for Gregory.

"Well, we're going to make paper airplanes, then," Ava said. "Bye, Gregory."

A soft alarm started to beep. A red ceiling light blinked. The ten mice sitting at the table jumped out of their seats.

A brown mouse burst into the room. He was shaking from head to tail. "We have a situation!"

"Of course. This is the Situation *Room*," Aunt Agnes said.

"No. This is serious. It has to do with a"—the mouse lowered his voice—"a . . . c-a-t!"